A TRIP TO ZIMBABWE WITH GOGO

SPIWE KACHIDZA-MAPFUMO

Copyright © 2022 by Spiwe Kachidza-Mapfumo
All rights reserved.
No part of this book may be reproduced in any form or by any electronic or mechanical means, including information storage and retrieval systems, without written permission from the author, except for the use of brief quotations in a book review.

DEDICATION

This book is dedicated to my grandchildren in Australia and all the Zimbabwean kids in the diaspora who wish to go and visit beautiful Zimbabwe, their parents' home country. My wish is to inspire kids to enjoy traveling and seeing the world.

This is the first of a series of books that will provide a window into what children can expect to see and experience when they visit Zimbabwe.

CONTENTS

1. Hwange trip with Gogo Mapfumo
2. Victoria Falls with Gogo
3. Going to Chiweshe village with Gogo.
4. Going to Mutoko with Gogo
5. A trip to Mbare Musika
6. Names and translations

CHAPTER 1
HWANGE TRIP WITH GOGO MAPFUMO

Gogo Mapfumo had spent 3 months visiting her son and his family Australia. She was going to take her grandchildren back to Zimbabwe on the kids' first trip to their father's home country. The preparation for the trip was exciting for the children. They had heard and read so much about the beautiful country of Zimbabwe.

A TRIP TO ZIMBABWE WITH GOGO

They also were looking forward to seeing their many cousins who they had not met before. Gogo promised to take them to Hwange on a safari where the kids would see the animals in the wild.

Makanaka the teenage granddaughter, Loyitso the boy, and the two younger grandkids Gamuchirai and Edzai could not wait for this amazing trip to Zimbabwe with their beloved Gogo. They were looking forward to seeing all these exciting places. When the day to leave for Zimbabwe arrived,

PAGE 2

HWANGE TRIP WITH GOGO MAPFUMO

their parents took them to Melbourne airport and off they were on this long journey to Africa with Gogo Mapfumo. When they arrived at Harare airport, they were met by their uncle Tapera. Uncle Tapera was so happy to meet the kids. Uncle Tapera Mapfumo was their paternal grandfather's young brother.

He loaded his car with the suitcases and bags and drove them to Gogo's house in Glen Lorne. They were excited to start their holiday and were ready to go visit the amazing places in Zimbabwe.

PAGE 3

A TRIP TO ZIMBABWE WITH GOGO

After two days of resting, Gogo told the kids that their three weeks holiday in Zimbabwe was going to start with a visit to the Hwange National Park and they were going to fly to Victoria Falls and then proceed to Hwange National Park.

They would come back to Victoria Falls and spend a day and a half seeing the famous mighty falls before returning to Harare. The four Mapfumo kids and Gogo packed their bags for the trip to Hwange.

HWANGE TRIP WITH GOGO MAPFUMO

Their uncle Tapera came to the house and loaded the bags into his car and drove them to the airport. He dropped them at the entrance of the domestic airport. Men, women, and children were all bustling around pulling their suitcases and bags. The kids and Gogo all thanked their uncle for driving them to the airport.

They waved at him as he drove off. Each of the kids pulled their bag following Gogo into the airport. Gogo went to one of the counters and checked in all their bags, showed the lady in a beautiful uniform their tickets.

A TRIP TO ZIMBABWE WITH GOGO

They were on their way to board Air Zimbabwe which was going to fly them to Victoria Falls. Gogo told her grandkids that they were going to land at Victoria Falls airport where they would rent a car that would take them to Hwange National Park.

When they got to Victoria Falls they picked their luggage and headed to the car rental desk and within a short time they put their backpacks in the 4x4 land cruiser and were off to Hwange. Gogo drove the car from the airport. She stopped at a store near the airport to buy water and cool drinks for them to take with them.

PAGE 6

HWANGE TRIP WITH GOGO MAPFUMO

When Gogo started the car, everyone was alert and very excited. The road to Hwange National Park was a beautiful tarred road with lush Musasa trees and the big fat baobab trees scattered in the bushes. As their car was driving on the road, they saw women with colorful dresses, carrying babies on their backs.

Some of the women were walking with big bags on their heads and some were selling stuff by the roadside.

PAGE 7

A TRIP TO ZIMBABWE WITH GOGO

They had lovely tablecloths in beautiful colors and various other items. There were some young men were standing next to the women, and they had various items and toy cars and tractors made of scrap metal and wire.

Loyiso was fascinated by the huge toy tractor complete with a John Deere logo stuck on it. He asked Gogo if he could buy the tractor and take it home. Gogo promised him that they will buy it on their way from Hwange as they had too much in the car.

PAGE 8

A TRIP TO ZIMBABWE WITH GOGO

After driving for an hour, they noticed a Hwange Safari Lodge sign and Gogo swung the car to the left of the road that led to the lodge where they were booked to stay. When they arrived, they parked the car in the parking lot and the kids carried their bags, following Gogo to the hotel reception. They were offered cool drinks and were shown their room which was overlooking the bush.

The lodge where they were going to sleep had two rooms and several beds enough for all of them.

HWANGE TRIP WITH GOGO MAPFUMO

After Gogo and her four grandchildren had lunch and rested, the sun was starting to go down. A big and tall African man dressed in khaki shorts and shirt and wearing a khaki bush hat came to the reception. He called out to the group who was waiting to go for the sunset drive to see the animals. There were some Americans who joined Gogo Mapfumo and her children. The kids put on their sunscreen put on their hats and were ready to go on a safari ride. Everybody boarded the open truck and Makanaka helped the kids to settle down.

PAGE 10

HWANGE TRIP WITH GOGO MAPFUMO

Loyiso, Gamuchirai, and Makanaka sat at the back between the tall American man and his wife and Edzai sat with behind the driver. Everybody was given a bottle of water to drink by the safari tour guide.

The truck drove through a bushy road and suddenly the driver stopped and everybody in the truck was asked to be quiet. They all watched the animal which was eating the leaves of a tree. The animal was brown, with beautiful patches on its skin, and had a very long neck. What animal was that?

PAGE 11

A TRIP TO ZIMBABWE WITH GOGO

Yes! It was a giraffe.

The driver started the car and drove on and again he suddenly stopped. He asked everyone to be quiet and watch on the right where there were many huge animals walking in a line with their babies. Even the babies were big! The animals were grey, and some had mud on them.

PAGE 12

HWANGE TRIP WITH GOGO MAPFUMO

They had long tusks and moved in a huge group going to a drinking hole. The tour guide told everyone that these animals move in herds, and they come down to the drinking hole to drink some water as it was very hot in that area.
What are those animals?

Elephants of course! As the driver started the truck some noise was coming from the trees nearby. A family of happy animals was swinging from branch to branch with their long tails waving in the air. What animals are these that swing from branch to branch?

Monkeys of course!

A TRIP TO ZIMBABWE WITH GOGO

The Americans who were in the car as well as Gogo were busy taking pictures while Makanaka, Loyiso, Gamuchirai, and Edzai, were looking out for more animals.

The sun was still hot, and the driver swung the car towards a river. By the banks of the river, they saw huge lizards basking in the sun. The lizards all looked like mud. They had what looked like scales all over their bodies and had large eyes that looked oily.

HWANGE TRIP WITH GOGO MAPFUMO

When the tour guide stopped the car closer to the river some snaked their way into the water leaving a wake behind them. The tour guide asked the kids what the name of the big lizards was. All four kids shouted Crocodile. After watching these crocodiles for a while, the tour driver got back on the road and headed back to the Lodge where they were going to have dinner and sleep.

When they arrived at the lodge, everybody got out of the truck and the kids headed to their rooms with Gogo.

PAGE 16

A TRIP TO ZIMBABWE WITH GOGO

They were all very hot and Gogo helped them with their cool evening baths and showers, then headed down to the bonfire for dinner with the rest of the tourists at that lodge.

After dinner, they put on their pajamas and went to bed. They were all worn out after a busy and exciting day. In the morning they ate breakfast, packed their backpacks, and headed back to Victoria Falls. They stopped at the road market and bought a big wire tractor for Loyiso from the young men who were selling

HWANGE TRIP WITH GOGO MAPFUMO

toys. Gogo drove back to Victoria Falls. They arrived at Victoria Falls and drove to A'zambezi Hotel where they were booked.

CHAPTER 2
VICTORIA FALLS WITH GOGO

After arriving in Victoria Falls and checking into A'zambezi Hotel, Gogo Mapfumo and her grandchildren, Makanaka, Loyiso, Gamuchirai, and Edzai, went to their hotel room. There were four beds in the room - one king-size bed and three single beds. Loyiso jumped on one of the single beds and Gamuchirai took another single bed while Makanaka put her satchel on the last one.

A TRIP TO ZIMBABWE WITH GOGO

Edzai jumped and held Gogo and declared that she was going to share the king-size bed with her. In the evening, they all went downstairs for dinner at the open restaurant. Many other tourists were already seated in the restaurant.

An African dance troupe was playing drums, singing, and dancing. Gogo, Makanaka, Loyiso, Gamuchirai, and Edzai sat around a table and watched the group perform.

PAGE 20

The dancers wore traditional clothing. The men wore an apron-like piece of cloth on their waist and traditional hats made of grass on their heads. They did not wear any shoes. The women had on short skirts in reds, blues and oranges.

A TRIP TO ZIMBABWE WITH GOGO

They each wore a headband with feathers in the front. They danced in a circle around the bonfire. Other tourists at the hotel also came down to have their dinner and to watch the dance troupe. Two young Americans joined the dancers and tried to follow what the dancing group was doing but the Americans couldn't follow the timing of the song.

Everyone started laughing and clapping to cheer them on. Everyone was having fun. Loyiso and his three sisters ordered hamburgers and chips, and Gogo ordered a steak and a glass of wine.

VICTORIA FALLS WITH GOGO

After eating dinner and cheering the dancers, Edzai was tired and sleepy. Gogo put her on her lap as she dozed off. Gogo and her grandchildren went back to their hotel room.

Everyone brushed their teeth, and Gogo put the mosquito nets over the kids' beds. Everyone was fast asleep in no time. It had been a long day for them all.

Early the next morning, the kids woke up and went to the balcony to see the beautiful Zambezi River. After Gogo got out of her bed, they all were ready for more fun.

A TRIP TO ZIMBABWE WITH GOGO

They went downstairs for breakfast. After breakfast, a big bus came to pick up all those who wanted to go on a tour of Victoria Falls. Gogo had bought tickets for all five of them.

All the kids put on their sunscreen with help from Makanaka. They wore their sunglasses, put on their sun hats, and jumped onto the tour bus. Gogo wore her big red sun hat, and they were all ready to see the famous Victoria Falls. The bus driver was a happy and chatty man. As he drove to the entrance of the Victoria Falls,

PAGE 24

he addressed his passengers using the loudspeaker. He told them the story of Victoria Falls and that its African name is *Mosi-o-Tunya*, which means "smoke that thunders" in the Kololo and Lozi languages. He told the tourists that the Lozi and Kololo people were the people who lived in that area many years ago before white people came to Zimbabwe.

The driver stopped the bus at the entrance of the falls and everybody jumped out and took turns to show their tickets to the lady at the entrance office.

A TRIP TO ZIMBABWE WITH GOGO

The kids were excited and Gogo paid for an umbrella and some raincoats for the kids. Then they got on the trail that led to the Falls through the rainforest. It always rains in the rainforest because of the water that falls into the gorge, the tour guide told everyone. All the tourists, including Gogo Mapfumo and her grandchildren walked through the bushes, and suddenly the majestic Victoria Falls was before them. The water roared down the cliff, sending particles of water into the sky to create something that looked like thick white smoke.

PAGE 26

VICTORIA FALLS WITH GOGO

The tour guide explained that the water flowed from another African country called Zambia. Gogo, Makanaka, Loyiso, Gamuchirai,and Edzai enjoyed seeing the spectacular Victoria Falls.

A TRIP TO ZIMBABWE WITH GOGO

They posed for pictures with the Victoria Falls in the background. The kids had promised their maternal grandmother and grandfather in Australia that they were going to take many pictures to show them all the places they visited in Zimbabwe.

They spent the whole day enjoying themselves and seeing many things around Victoria falls. The tour guide took the group to the bridge that crossed over to Zambia. There they saw men, women, and other young people bungee jumping.

VICTORIA FALLS WITH GOGO

They tied a safety belt to their waists, jumped into the raging Zambezi River, and suddenly swooped back up to the bridge. It looked scary, but Loyiso told Gogo that when he turned fifteen, he would like to come back and bungee jump like those tourists were doing.

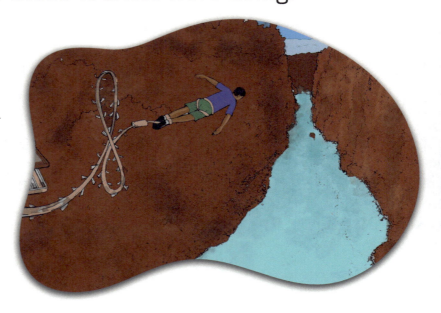

A TRIP TO ZIMBABWE WITH GOGO

After the morning trip to see Victoria Falls, they were driven back to the hotel where they had lunch and went to their room to lie down and rest. Makanaka did not sleep; instead, she read a Shona dictionary that Gogo bought for her. She was keen on learning the language spoken by her relatives in Zimbabwe.

At about four p.m. Gogo woke the kids, and they all went downstairs for a boat cruise down the Zambezi River. At the riverside, they jumped into the boat with other tourists.

PAGE 30

VICTORIA FALLS WITH GOGO

The kids sat down on a bench next to Gogo. She was wearing her red hat which she wore everywhere they went. The captain started the boat engine and they started sailing down the big Zambezi River.

An African song boomed from the speakers on the boat. There was a small bar at the front of the boat and a skinny man was selling drinks to the people on the boat. Everyone bought some drinks and Gogo bought some for her grandchildren.

PAGE 31

A TRIP TO ZIMBABWE WITH GOGO

Makanaka ordered an orange juice, Loyiso wanted Fanta while Gamuchirai and Edzai wanted cherry plum. As the boat went down the Zambezi River, the kids sat patiently and happily sipped their drinks whilst watching the water flow downstream.

Suddenly the boat driver turned off the engine and asked everyone to look towards the banks of the river to their left. There along the banks were five huge crocodiles basking in the setting sun. They had their babies, the tiny crocodiles, with them.

PAGE 32

VICTORIA FALLS WITH GOGO

People started taking pictures of the crocodiles. Suddenly the crocodiles swam into the river leaving a wake behind. The boat continued down the river for another hour as the tourists enjoyed the setting sun.

A TRIP TO ZIMBABWE WITH GOGO

Occasionally a hippo would swim close to the boat and the tourists would take pictures and cheer for the hippo. Everyone on the boat was in awe of the animals. Suddenly right next to the boat there in the middle of the river, a flurry of water came out through the nose of a hippo swimming near the boat. Loyiso, Gamuchirai, and Edzai were first startled, but they soon joined the rest of the tourists to cheer the hippos.

After a while, the hippo swam away and the boat captain turned on the engine,

PAGE 34

turned the boat around, and headed back to the hotel. When they arrived, they all got out of the boat and headed to the open restaurant for dinner. They all sat down in the sitting area where dinner was served.

They watched another group of dancers playing their drums and singing and clapping around the bonfire. After dinner, they went to their room, showered, put on their pyjamas, and went to sleep. In the morning, the kids packed their bags and their satchels and Gogo drove them back

A TRIP TO ZIMBABWE WITH GOGO

to the airport for their flight back to Harare. At the airport, Gogo returned the car to the rental office, and they checked in at the Air Zimbabwe counter.

VICTORIA FALLS WITH GOGO

Loyiso's big wire tractor, which they bought by the roadside from Hwange, was nicely packed in a big box. Gogo checked it in with the rest of the luggage. Loyiso asked the luggage man if he could put a red sticker with the word FRAGILE written on it on the box so it would not be crushed. He was happy when the luggage man agreed to let him do that. They boarded the evening flight back to Harare.

They had such a wonderful time in Victoria Falls and Hwange Safari.

PAGE 37

CHAPTER 3
GOING TO CHIWESHE VILLAGE WITH GOGO

Makanaka and the other kids all thanked Gogo for the exciting visit to the amazing and famous Victoria Falls and for the opportunity to go on a safari holiday. The Tuesday after Gogo and the kids returned from the exciting trip to Hwange Safari and the Victoria Falls, Gogo told the kids that the next visit was to Chiweshe village where their father grew up.

A TRIP TO ZIMBABWE WITH GOGO

The village is about forty-five minutes from Glen Lorne where Gogo Mapfumo lives. Early in the morning, the kids had packed their bags with gifts they had brought from Australia to give to their cousins whom they had never met. Gogo packed boxes with some food, bread, meat, drinks, biscuits, and sweets which she was taking to the village.

After they had their breakfast, they all jumped into Gogo's car, and they left for Sam Levy shopping center to fill up the car with fuel.

GOING TO CHIWESHE VILLAGE WITH GOGO

From the filling station, Gogo started the car and drove to Ashdown Park to pick gogo Mwela who was going to accompany them to Chiweshe. *Gogo* Mwela was the younger sister to their late great-grandmother.

As matriarch, she played a very important role in the Mapfumo family. The kids were happy to see *gogo* Mwela again. She had once visited Australia and stayed in their home. The kids gave *gogo* Mwela a beautiful handbag that they had brought for her from Australia.

PAGE 40

A TRIP TO ZIMBABWE WITH GOGO

She clapped in appreciation as is done in the Shona culture. Everyone got into the car and Gogo Mapfumo started driving towards Mazowe, a dam along the way to Chiweshe village.

gogo Mwela, a retired teacher, told the three kids about their family and village life. She told them how she and her siblings used to walk for miles to school when she was a little girl and how they had so much fun with her friends in the village. Little Edzai asked *gogo* Mwela why her mother did not drop her at school with the car as her parents did.

PAGE 41

GOING TO CHIWESHE VILLAGE WITH GOGO

Gogo Mwela laughed and told Edzai that her parents did not have a car and all the children in the village walked to school together in the morning. After driving for twenty minutes, they got to Mazowe Dam where they stopped to buy bags of oranges at a kiosk to take with them to the village.

Makanaka arranged the bags of oranges in the car and gave each of the kids fresh-squeezed orange juice that Gogo had bought for them.

A TRIP TO ZIMBABWE WITH GOGO

After twenty five more minutes of driving towards the homestead where their cousins lived, they arrived at an open field, just by a small river. *Gogo* Mwela pointed to the boys who were herding cattle in the field.

She told the Mapfumo kids that the boys in the village went out to care for the cattle while the girls stayed at home helping the mothers with housework and fetching water from the well. Gogo Mapfumo turned to the right and drove down a dirt road that would take them to the village.

PAGE 43

GOING TO CHIWESHE VILLAGE WITH GOGO

They drove past some round houses with nicely thatched roofs. Some of the huts looked like the ones they had seen at Hwange Safari lodge. The village women who were sitting on mats on the ground recognized Gogo's car and waved at them. Loyiso and his sisters waved back and asked if Gogo knew the women. Gogo told them that they were relatives, and they knew her car that was why they were waving at them.

Gogo drove slowly through a shallow stream, and just after that stream,

PAGE 44

they saw some kids who were playing soccer, while cattle were drinking water from the stream. Loyiso was excited as he loves playing soccer.

The boys were playing with a ball made from plastic. They all looked very happy. *Gogo* Mwela told Loyiso that those boys were his cousins who lived in the village. Finally, they arrived at the homestead where *mbuya mai* Sydney lived. They all got out of the car and *mbuya mai* Sydney and the girls at the homestead came out

GOING TO CHIWESHE VILLAGE WITH GOGO

ululating, dancing, and singing to welcome the Mapfumo kids. After the warm reception, they all went into the house and *mbuya mai* Sydney asked her older granddaughter Tabitha to go catch two chickens and cook them for their guests.

All the kids at the house started running around the homestead after the chicken. Makanaka the teenager, Loyiso, Gamuchirai, and little Edzai all joined their cousins in the chase. After a while, the children caught two chickens and took them to the kitchen

A TRIP TO ZIMBABWE WITH GOGO

where they were prepared for the visitors. While the cooking was going on, Loyiso and his cousins from the village pitched a makeshift soccerfield.

Loyiso went to Gogo Mapfumo and asked for the soccer ball he had brought from Australia.

His cousins were elated that they were going to kick a real leather soccer ball. They started playing soccer, scoring into the makeshift goalposts.

PAGE 47

GOING TO CHIWESHE VILLAGE WITH GOGO

When the food was ready, the kids were asked to wash their hands and each child was given a plate of sadza, chicken, green vegetables, and lots of gravy. All the boys sat under the mango tree in the homestead to eat their lunch. The girls sat with the women in the sitting room.

A TRIP TO ZIMBABWE WITH GOGO

Makanaka helped their cousins to bring plates of *sadza* to everyone in the room and sat next to Edzai and Gamuchirai.

Gogo Mwela prayed for the food before starting to eat. Edzai told Gogo Mapfumo that she enjoyed the chicken and that it was different from the one they ate at home. After eating, Loyiso asked if he could go out for a while with his cousins to herd the cattle. *Mbuya mai* Sydney nodded her approval and gave all the boys drinks before they went out to bring the cattle back to the homestead. Makanaka, Gamuchirai, and Edzai helped to wash the dishes outside the kitchen.

The older cousins who prepared the food showed them how to rinse the dishes in clean water and put them on a table to dry. Soon after, *mbuya mai* Sidney took some peanuts and roasted them. The children took out the gifts that they had brought. They gave *mbuya mai* Sydney a beautiful blanket. She clapped her hands and started ululating, thanking them for the gift.

A TRIP TO ZIMBABWE WITH GOGO

They gave a t-shirt to their cousin Tabitha who cooked for them and gave the boys t-shirts with pictures of Kangaroos on them. Loyiso also gave them the football. Everybody was excited and happy. Just as the sun began to set, the boys and Loyiso came back with the cattle. They gave the Mapfumo kids and their *Gogo* peanuts to take back to Harare. *Gogo* Mapfumo quickly came out of the house to take a picture of Loyiso and his cousins driving the cattle into the kraal for the night. Soon after, it was time to get back to Harare.

PAGE 51

GOING TO CHIWESHE VILLAGE WITH GOGO

Gogo Mapfumo and the kids thanked everyone, said their farewells, got into the car and began their journey back to Harare. They dropped *gogo* Mwela off at her house in Ashdown Park before going to Gogo's place in Glen Lorne.

CHAPTER 4
GOING TO MUTOKO WITH GOGO

Gogo Mapfumo was excited to take her visiting grandchildren to Mutoko, the place where she was born and raised.

On a beautiful Sunday morning, they woke up and had breakfast. The grandchildren packed their bags and loaded everything into Gogo's car.

A TRIP TO ZIMBABWE WITH GOGO

They had brought some gifts from Australia to give to more relatives in Mutoko.

Like the highways in Australia, the road to Mutoko was beautiful and busy. There were big trucks, small cars, and buses overtaking one another on the road.

A TRIP TO ZIMBABWE WITH GOGO

Along the main road were women walking with babies on their backs and buckets balanced on their heads.

A man was riding a bicycle with a big hessian bag at the back of the bicycle with an animal's head sticking out of the sack. The kids were amused to see the man riding a bicycle with a live animal on the bike.

Gamuchirai asked Gogo to slow down so they could see what animal was in the sack. The kids, with their eyes wide open, shouted that it looked like a dog.

PAGE 55

GOING TO MUTOKO WITH GOGO

"No! It's a goat," they all shouted after Gogo slowed down the car.

Gogo told the kids that the man might be taking the goat to the next small township to sell so that he could have money to buy food for his family.

They finally got to Mutoko and Gogo drove to the house where they were met by their aunt *ambuya mai wa* Sam and *mbuya* Mudzinga and another *gogo*.

A TRIP TO ZIMBABWE WITH GOGO

They were all sitting on a mat under the mango tree outside the house.

Mbuya mai Sam was happy to see Gogo and the children.

She started to sing a song of welcome for them. The other two aunts also joined in the ululation, singing, and clapping.

Mauya mauya mauya wana wemuzukuru wangu.

Mauya mauya masvika mumusha medu wazukuru.

Aiwa nhasi wana sekuru wachauraya mbudzi kufarira wazukuru.

Mauya mauya nhasi tese tinofara.

GOING TO MUTOKO WITH GOGO

Gogo Mapfumo joined in the singing and the kids joined in the clapping. After the singing, chairs were brought out for them to sit.

Makanaka went with the other kids back to the car to fetch the parcels they had brought for their *Mbuya.*

They brought out a lovely blanket and a handbag that their mother bought for *mbuya ma*i Sam. They also gave the other two aunts some headscarves. After a short while, Gogo's brother, *sekuru* Fungai, arrived at the house with another uncle. He was happy to see Gogo and the Mapfumo kids.

A TRIP TO ZIMBABWE WITH GOGO

The uncles told them that they had brought a goat, which they were going to slaughter and prepare for them.

Sekuru Fungai said it was a special custom in Mutoko to slaughter a goat when grandchildren from far away came to visit for the first time.

The two men went to the back of the house, slaughtered the goat and hung it on a tree branch. They then called the kids to come and see how they would open the stomach of the goat with sharp knives and pull out all the insides into a big dish. They took out the intestines, the liver, and the tripe. Edzai asked what that towel-like-looking piece in the dish was called.

A TRIP TO ZIMBABWE WITH GOGO

Sekuru Fungai told the kids that it was called *guru*, which is the stomach of the goat. Loyiso ran back to tell Gogo that they had seen *sekuru* Fungai cutting out meat from the goat. He had never seen that in Australia. *Sisi* Abi, the lady who was helping *mbuya mai* Sam to cook for the guests, came out of the house, took the dish, and started cleaning the

PAGE 60

A TRIP TO ZIMBABWE WITH GOGO

pieces of meat that were brought out of the goat's stomach. After all the meat was cleaned and ready, *sisi* Abi made small sausage-like pieces from the tripe or *guru* wrapping around it the long intestines. All these *maguru*, which is tripe, were put in a big pot separate from the rest of the goat meat and started to cook on a fireplace.

Later when it was well cooked, *sisi* Abi added onions and tomatoes to make the stew. Most of the meat was cut into pieces and taken into the house where it was cooked and there was more stew,

PAGE 61

GOING TO MUTOKO WITH GOGO

and the rest was roasted over a fire that the men had set up outside near where the goat was slaughtered. The roasted meat was placed on a plate, and it was given to everyone who was there to eat. The grandchildren loved the roasted goat meat.

When the *guru* and the meat were nicely cooked and a big pot of *sadza* was made, *mbuya mai* Sam served everybody and she asked *gogo* Mudzinga to pray before they ate the food. She started the prayer by thanking God for Gogo Mapfumo who brought the

A TRIP TO ZIMBABWE WITH GOGO

grandchildren to see the relatives in Mutoko. She prayed for the Mapfumo kids' parents in Australia, prayed for those who slaughtered the goat and those who cooked the food.

She then prayed that the children and Gogo Mapfumo travel well to Harare and the kids back to Australia.

It was a long prayer for the hungry kids. Edzai, who was getting tired of closing her eyes during the long prayer opened one eye and saw that Loyiso was also opening his eyes.

GOING TO MUTOKO WITH GOGO

Both children were hungry and ready to eat. When *mbuya* Mudzinga finally finished praying, they all washed their hands, clapped their hands as they were taught by Gogo Mapfumo, and started eating the delicious *sadza* and goat intestines that *sisi* Abi had prepared.

After everyone finished eating, the kids went outside the house with *sisi* Abi and helped her get mangoes from the many trees around the homestead. She took a long tree branch and they went from tree to tree shaking the mangoes down.

PAGE 64

GOING TO MUTOKO WITH GOGO

The kids washed the ripe mangoes. They were orange in color and very juicy. *sisi* Abi moved to another tree, which had big green mangoes she called Bull mangoes.

A TRIP TO ZIMBABWE WITH GOGO

Makanaka, Loyiso and the other two kids helped pick the mangoes they had felled from the tree and packed them in a cardboard box to take back to Harare.

Gogo thanked *mbuya mai* Sam, *gogo* Mudzinga and her friend as well for welcoming them. She also thanked *sekuru* Fungai for slaughtering the goat and welcoming the Mapfumo kids to their Gogo's rural home.

GOING TO MUTOKO WITH GOGO

Gogo gave the two *sekurus* some money to go buy themselves some beer. She also gave *gogo* Mudzinga and her friend some gifts she had brought for them.

It was time to say their goodbyes and head back to Harare. Gogo started the car, and they began their journey back home. On the road, they saw buses with loads of stuff on their roofs. The buses were going much faster than Gogo's car.

PAGE 67

A TRIP TO ZIMBABWE WITH GOGO

There were sacks, suitcases, bags, and boxes full of red tomatoes and some with mangoes. Gogo told the kids that these boxes with vegetables and fruit were going to Mbare Musika to be sold to people in the city, and she promised to take the grandchildren on a tour of the big market. Every so often a bus would pass them and it would stop at a station to pick or drop people.

Women were carrying babies on their backs, men and children stood outside the bus calling out for their parcels to be

GOING TO MUTOKO WITH GOGO

handed to them by a man who was at the top of the bus. Some of the women, men, and children were selling mangoes, tomatoes, cucumbers, and many other fruits and vegetables to people on the bus. All the people were screaming out what they were selling and the people in the bus would buy fruit and vegetables; they paid for the fruits and vegetables that they bought through the bus window.

The bus driver honked and all the people selling stuff ran off from the bus

PAGE 69

A TRIP TO ZIMBABWE WITH GOGO

just before the driver pulled out of the station. They drove back to Gogo's house in Glen Lorne and mukoma Shemu, the gardener, came out to help them get all the boxes with mangoes from Mutoko into the house. The kids were tired but they wanted to eat a few more mangoes that *mbuya mai* Sam had packed for them. They washed their hands and started eating more mangoes.

They gave some of the mangoes to Mukoma Shemu to eat with his family.

GOING TO MUTOKO WITH GOGO

It was a great visit to Mutoko where Gogo Mapfumo was born and raised.Gogo promised the kids that she was going to take them to Mbare musika, a huge market in one of the high-density areas where a lot of Zimbabweans live.

CHAPTER 5
A TRIP TO MBARE MUSIKA

On a Saturday morning, Gogo Mapfumo told her grandchildren to get ready for a visit to Mbare musika as she had promised them. She told her grandkids that Mbare was one of Harare's oldest townships. Since their arrival in Zimbabwe from Australia, the children had visited Victoria Falls, Hwange Safari, the village in

A TRIP TO ZIMBABWE WITH GOGO

Chiweshe where they met a lot of their cousins, and Mutoko where Gogo was born and raised. It was going to be another hot day. The kids could feel it even though it was still early in the morning. After breakfast, Gogo reminded the kids to apply sunscreen on their faces and put on their sun hats.

After doing that, they were ready to go to the Mbare market. They all jumped into Gogo's car. *Mukoma* Shemu, the gardener at Gogo Mapfumo's house,

PAGE 73

A TRIP TO MBARE MUSIKA

sat in the front passenger seat with Gogo, while the four grandchildren sat in the back seat. *Mukoma* Shemu would look after the car while Gogo and the kids went inside the market.

Gogo didn't want to fall victim to the petty thieves around the market who break into people's cars to steal.
Gogo Mapfumo packed some bags of bananas that she had earlier picked from the huge banana tree in her compound. She put the bags under the back seat.

A TRIP TO ZIMBABWE WITH GOGO

After putting her red sun hat on, she pulled out onto the road and drove to Mbare through the city center.

They stopped at a traffic light and three kids came to Gogo's window with their hands out asking for money. Loyiso asked Gogo what the kids in the street wanted. She locked the doors and asked Makanaka to wind up the windows.

Gogo Mapfumo pulled out the bag of bananas from under the back seat and gave a bunch to the street kids.

PAGE 75

A TRIP TO MBARE MUSIKA

They stopped at a traffic light and three kids came to Gogo's window with their hands out asking for money.

A TRIP TO ZIMBABWE WITH GOGO

They drove through the city where they saw lots of people walking about. Some of the people were selling phone cards, cell phones, and all sorts of things.

After several stops at traffic lights, Gogo gave out more bananas to kids asking for help. They drove under the flyover that led directly to Mbare *musika*.

Within a few more minutes, they were at the Mbare market. The children saw many people involved in different activities.

A TRIP TO MBARE MUSIKA

Some of them were sitting way up on top of lorries arriving at the market with boxes piled high up into the sky.

These lorries looked like the ones they saw on their way from Mutoko. Some of the lorries were carrying cabbages, tomatoes and some had mangoes. Gogo told them that farmers brought these vegetables to sell to people in the city.

Gogo Mapfumo told her grandkids that Mbare was the oldest township in Harare. She told the kids that many of the people in Harare lived in high-density townships. She explained to them that a long time before Zimbabwe was a free country,

A TRIP TO MBARE MUSIKA

Africans lived in Mbare and were not allowed to live in places like Glen Lorne where Gogo Mapfumo now lived. She also told them that the market had been there for many years.

Gogo took her grandkids round the Mbare market. She wanted them to see what the market looked like. There were so many people selling all sorts of things in the market. Some were selling fruits, vegetables such as carrots, cabbages, tomatoes and cucumbers, and many other food items that the kids did not know.

A TRIP TO ZIMBABWE WITH GOGO

It sounded like all the traders were calling out to people to come and buy their stuff. An old woman was selling African dolls dressed in colorful African clothes.

Gogo also bought some sweet potatoes, and Edzai asked Gogo if she could have an African doll. Gogo bought the two young grandkids African dolls. She bought Makanaka a sunhat in African print. They were all happy. The four grandchildren remembered to say *mazvita* to all the people they bought stuff from as Gogo

PAGE 81

A TRIP TO MBARE MUSIKA

had taught them earlier. *Mazvita* means thank you in the Shona language. After going around the market, they went back to their car where *mukoma* Shemu was waiting. They packed everything they bought in the car and Gogo started them on their journey back home.

They stopped for a while at Chisipite, a smaller market in the area. There, they saw women carrying babies on their backs selling colorful tablecloths. The men were selling wooden and stone sculptures.

A TRIP TO ZIMBABWE WITH GOGO

There was also a flower market where men rushed to Gogo's car calling out to her to buy their flowers. They also saw some boys selling cars made from wire like the one Gogo bought for Loyiso in Hwange. Gogo bought two tablecloths which had animals on them. She chose one with Zimbabwe's "The Big Five" animals, which are elephant, leopard, lion, buffalo, and rhino. One tablecloth was for the kids' mother, the other was for their grandmother in Australia. Gogo also bought some wall hangings with the Victoria Falls painted on them

PAGE 83

A TRIP TO MBARE MUSIKA

and another one with pictures of African women with babies on their back like the women who were selling at the market.

Some white people who looked like tourists also arrived in a car. As soon as the other car arrived all the sellers rushed to that car with their stuff. After their shopping, they all went back into the car and headed home. When they got home, *mukoma* Shemu helped take the stuff they had bought into the house.

They were all excited, and they started playing with the toys that Gogo had bought for them.

A TRIP TO ZIMBABWE WITH GOGO

Gamuchirai named her doll Rudo, a Shona name meaning love, and Edzai named her doll Chipo, a Shona name meaning gift. They thanked Gogo for taking them to Mbare *musika*. Gogo told the kids that they were going to start packing and getting ready for them to go back to Australia.

She has shown them a small part of Zimbabwe and she was hoping they were going to come back with their parents' next time. Gogo was not going back to Australia with the kids but was going to stay behind.

PAGE 85

A TRIP TO MBARE MUSIKA

The kids were joining another uncle who was returning to Melbourne where he lived. Gogo packed all the children's bags and made sure they took all the gifts they had bought for their parents and their friends. Makanaka was excited because she had learned a few Shona words and she could say a few sentences in Shona.

She put her Shona dictionary in her handbag so that she could check the words. The day of leaving Zimbabwe arrived and three weeks had gone so fast. The kids have a wonderful time with Gogo.

PAGE 86

A TRIP TO ZIMBABWE WITH GOGO

When she drove them to the airport to meet their father's friend uncle Zorodzo and his wife aunt Philana and their 2 little girls Sia and Mali who were all flying back to Melbourne. They all huddled around Gogo and did not want to leave her. She gave them hugs and kisses and they went into the departure lounge with their uncle and aunt and still waving at Gogo.

PAGE 81

SHORT BIO ABOUT THE AUTHOR

Spiwe Kachidza-Mapfumo is a journalist, vlogger, writer, and broadcaster. A world traveler, Spiwe has visited many countries.

Born in Mutoko, Zimbabwe, she went to the United States of America for her university education. She graduated from Iowa State University in Journalism and Mass Communication.

After university, she moved back to Zimbabwe where she worked as a journalist and in Public Relations for many years. In 2005 Spiwe moved to Canada.

She now lives in Calgary, Alberta. Spiwe has one son and 4 grandchildren who all live in Melbourne Australia.

NAMES AND TRANSLATIONS

Gogo - Grandmother gogo - an elderly aunt

Guru - Tripe

Mukoma - big brother /a male househelp

Sisy - big sister/female househelp

Mbuya - an aunt

Mai wa Sam - the mother of Sam (An aunt)

Mai wa Sydney - the mother of Sydney (An aunt)

Musika - Market

Sekuru - Uncle

CREDITS
Illustrator - Hennings Masikati
Edits - Aisha Ostberg

Manufactured by Amazon.ca
Bolton, ON

24684671R00052